A RECORD IN SPACE

Writings by the 2015-2016 826CHI
Youth Advisory Board

826CHI

MOODY PUBLICATIONS

IN CONJUNCTION WITH 826CHI

CHICAGO

MOODY PUBLICATIONS

IN CONJUNCTION WITH 826CHI 1276 N. MILWAUKEE AVE-
NUE, CHICAGO, IL 60622, USA

A RECORD IN SPACE

Our gratitude, however, is not a work of fiction, and is in this instance bestowed thusly: to Delia Jean Hickey for illustrating this book's beautiful cover, and to Gage Salzano, for the typesetting and layout design of the manuscript. We would also like to thank 826CHI volunteers Ashley Kolpak, Chelsea McDonald, Brandan Baki, and Amanda Nyren, for supporting the Youth Advisory Board throughout the academic year.

Proceeds from the sale of this publication support 826CHI, a non-profit creative writing, tutoring, and publishing center.
www.826chi.org

FIRST ED. 826CHI 2016 • PRINTED IN CHICAGO, IL

CONTENTS

*　　*　　*

CONTENTS CONTINUED.

*   *   *

FOREWORD

Ladan Osman

The 826CHI Youth Advisory Board demonstrates facility in storytelling and dedication to crafting images specific to their experiences. When I visited as a teaching artist, it was a real pleasure to encounter their thoughtful responses, starting with check-in questions and teaser prompts. They shared their fears, morning rituals, and aspirations, and their words have stayed with me, have appeared in my dreams. "A Record in Space" incorporates origination myths, and makes the everyday fantastic.

The use of color and light is striking. In each piece, the reader's eye is encouraged to move from line to line. This aesthetic attentiveness also exists conceptually. These writers address war, forced migration, social isolation, the tension between private and public persona, and conflict with external expectations. They write about loneliness and comfort with isolation, and create myths for these speakers: they observe or apply magic, they are terrible or they are average and grappling with common concerns.

These writings pursue images: warmth of bread, light through a window, notes playing in a room, wind moving across a body. Whether in fiction or poetry, these voices are direct and speak of serious intentions. One of the most fascinating elements is the relationship between the surreal and the real. These works brim with emotion and detail pressure on these speakers and characters. At any time, a voice may break out of reality and enter a speculative space. I believe this comes from deep engagement with a present moment, facing the available world, then describing or improving upon it using language and image. I invite you to read and reread these rising writers and to fully engage with their worlds.

HELLO!

Welcome to the 2015-2016 Youth Advisory Board chapbook, *A Record in Space.*

The 826CHI Youth Advisory Board (YAB) is a collective of high school students from various Chicago schools that meets biweekly to share writing and thoughts about literature. We travel through rain or snow to meet at 826CHI on Monday evenings for a creative writing workshop that culminates in the production of a chapbook featuring original work. YAB serves as a safe, empowering environment for young writers, a designated time for writing freely and sharing with a community of like-minded peers. It is a space where writing is valued and taken seriously.

While members of the general public must be at least 18 years old in order to volunteer at 826CHI, YAB members are given the opportunity to participate in the organization's programs as tutors and mentors for younger students. The service component of the workshop offers an introduction to volunteering and 826CHI's mission: to support students with their creative and expository writing skills. YAB also serves as a cohort of ambassadors for 826CHI by representing the organization at literary events across the city.

This year, we read poetry, essays, and short fiction by Ann Beattie, John Cheever, Tavi Gevinson, Zadie Smith, Nate Marshall, and Tyler Ford, among others. Many of us were encountering these writers for the first time, exploring themes and styles that we were unfamiliar with during our group discussions. We decided against setting a theme for this chapbook and opted for the freedom to tell a range of stories inspired by the diverse voices represented on our reading list.

We would like to thank Tracy Woodley and Amanda Lichtenstein, for leading YAB and providing a space for us to excel; 826CHI volunteers Ashley Kolpak, Chelsea McDonald, Amanda Nyren, and Brandan Baki for listening to us, encouraging us, and for proofreading and copyediting the manuscript of our chapbook; Ladan Osman, for visiting us twice to share her work and discuss the writing process, and for writing the foreword to our book; Brian Martin, for leading a powerful guest workshop on personal narratives; Delia Jean Hickey, for creating the beautiful cover art for our book; and

Gage Salzano, for typesetting this manuscript and designing
the interior layout of this chapbook.

So, here it is– the culmination of 19 workshop sessions over
the course of an entire school year. We hope you enjoy our
collection. As you read, remember that everything is *a record in
space.*

– THE 2015-2016 YOUTH ADVISORY BOARD

LOST SAVE

Aphra Price

This evening, you are waiting for your friend on a busy sidewalk, in front of a storefront that trumpets, "WE FIX BROKEN GAME CONSOLES." You have a dull headache, and there is a slight warm rain drizzling on your shoulders. You look down to check your watch, then notice that you no longer have a watch on— although you're very certain you did at some point. You hear your phone ring, playing the default tone that you never figured out how to change.

You twist around and reach into your shoulder bag, but you cannot find your phone. In fact, your bag is empty except for your house keys, which are almost swallowed by the logo-patterned silk lining. You pick up the keys and jingle them, still in your awkward, half-turned position. When you put the keys back in your purse, you realize that the phone was there all along. You turn it on, and see that your friend is twenty minutes late. You go to her contact information (she is represented by a picture of a sleeping cat), and call, hearing thirty seconds of her mariachi ringtone before she picks up.

"Heyyy...sorry I'm late, yeah well, I'm gonna be like another *hour*, at least," she says. You grimace widely, and breathe out through your teeth.

"Oh. Um...I actually, really can't wait that long," you reply.

"Oh my gosh, sorry!" she shouts, making your shoulders tense up.

"Y-yes. Got to go home, get some work done," you say. You do have a lot of things to *do*, but you don't remember them at the moment. Your responsibilities have melded into many text-coated stacks of paper, which are held together with staples and binder clips and thread.

"Maybe I'll swing by later, yeah?" she says.

"Yes. Good. Good idea. See you then, well, maybe," you say. You hang up and sigh loudly, since your friend can no longer hear you. You have known her since you were six years old, and she has never once been punctual. But you can't bring yourself to show up late, and so you're always on time, sometimes early. This is the first day in recent memory that you haven't waited for her, and it's mostly because you are getting damp. Some days you wonder whether you have any guts at all.

When you return to your address, your home has been replaced by an empty concrete lot, surrounded by a chainlink fence and occupied solely by a red office chair. Its shiny pleather cushion cover is almost entirely shredded, showcasing the moldy, yellowish foam underneath. You could've sworn there was a house here before. No, you know there was a house here before. But when you try to picture it, it doesn't work. It's yellow. No, it's green. You don't know. A knot twists in your throat, and you start breathing harder. You are imitating panic the way you've seen it on TV, shaking like a leaf because you know that's what you are meant to do, and because it is the only familiar thing in a totally foreign situation. You choke out a hopeless yell that sounds like a bad recording of you, and hit the fence. Then you wince and rub your knuckles. Even though you can see that the fence is locked and rusted shut, you begin rattling it. Fifty-three seconds later, you give up.

You try to grab the top of the fence, extending yourself to your full height. You still believe that the empty lot is a product of your spiteful mind, and that if you could only get inside the lot, you would *feel* the house and know you had lied to yourself. So you jump maniacally up and down like a desperate fan trying to see the stage at a concert. You finally do grab on, and hold on despite the cold, biting feel of the metal. You jam one grimy sneaker into the fence's loose steel weave, and then raise another hand.

Once you find space for your other foot, you pull yourself up, and lose a shoe doing so. Your stomach has landed on the prongs of the fence, and you wheeze loudly. You tilt forward, and when you try to steady yourself the pain in your abdomen increases. Then you bring up one knee, and slam it into the fence over and over while gripping the metal just barely harder than you thought you could. Finally, you manage to bring one leg over the top, stabbing the edge of the fence into the crook of your knee. You wince, but swing over your other leg, moving your arms to accommodate your new position. Then you drop down, letting out a short, desperate noise.

You contemplate taking out your phone and calling for help. To a hospital, maybe, somewhere where they could explain this away as a disease in your spine, your brain, something insidious creeping into your bone marrow. There could be a cure, a hope, and after therapy and effort, a complete return to normalcy. Employees will wheel you out one day to your cheering family. You realize you cannot remember clearly the faces of your family, only the friend who was too late to meet you today. You begin to cry, but only a few tears drip out before you are finished. You keep making noises, and it is as if you are pumping a spray bottle that refuses to work. But you know it's not empty.

Even if the sickness cannot be eradicated, you at least want to know it exists. An excuse, a doctor's note, a lifting and unspooling of responsibility that will leave you to a quiet life under smooth floral-and-cream sheets. Perhaps sometimes you will even have moments of clarity. You reach for your phone, and it is now you realize that your bag is gone, and has been since you placed your hands on the fence. You don't remember taking it off. You didn't take it off. You don't have your phone, your house keys... or your *house*, for that matter. You think you remember getting out of bed this morning, but that too is blurred now, just like your work. A geometrically patterned comforter, stinging eyes, and the default tone of your alarm clock that you never figured out how to change.

"Hey!" says the voice of a stranger. "If it helps any, it was never really yours to begin with!"

"Are you— are you talking to me?" you ask, even though you are the only person within earshot.

"Yes, yes I am! I'm talking about your house," says the stranger, who is stepping closer. You do not know why he came here.

"I... it's really gone? Where is it?" you say, turning your head as much as you can. The stranger is tall and bony, with dark eyes. He carries a large, drab, olive-colored bag, and speaks with an accent that almost sounds British, but is in fact just an odd tone of voice. You are certain that you don't know this man,

but he reminds you of some acquaintance you never liked,
although you aren't sure who. Possibly a friend of your parents
who smoked in front of you, or a fellow student who always
slurped green tea and filled out a crossword during lectures.
You are yourself a crossword being done in reverse, a video
played backwards. Every stroke of ink is dissolved until only
the silent black squares remain.

"I don't know where the house is, sorry," he says. "Should have
said that to begin with. You don't get a phone number to call
about it. Because. You no longer have a phone."

"I don't. You know what's happening? You know what this
is?" you ask. You are dizzy, and the outside world looks
blurry to you.

"It's all going to be given back," says the stranger. "Like I said,
none of these things belonged to you. You didn't earn them, but
you were supposed to. It's all— it's all cogs, you know? Plans.
Stuff you didn't live up to." He is leaning on the fence now,
peering at you.

"I don't understand." you say.

"Why did you climb over the fence? What did you even think
that would do?" You can clearly see it's just an empty lot here,"
the stranger says. He rattles the fence, and then starts kicking
it. You cringe at the noise.

"It's not empty!" you shout. You are fully aware that this is a lie,
but you are hoping somehow your statement will change this.
It reminds you of a dream you had once, where you were trying
to teleport from a train station onto a train. You knew you

had teleported earlier, and had done it many times in the past, though you couldn't understand how anymore. You focused on the train very hard, and you didn't know what you were doing wrong, but you could *feel* it not happening. This is that feeling.

"What, the office chair? That doesn't mean anything," he says. Your face gets hot, and you square your shoulders. You feel an instinct to defend your home, or lack thereof.

"Quit kicking the fence, it's *rusted shut*!" you shriek. The stranger jerks his leg backward, and falls off balance doing so. He almost topples over, but then he throws his skinny arms outward like wings, and somehow catches himself on nothing.

"I know that! I'm frustrated, all right? You're being very frustrating," he says.

"You... I..." you try to say. You want to tell him he has no right to be frustrated, that obviously you are the one with real problems here. But three whole outbursts? Two is more than enough— that put you over your limit already. You are weak.

"Listen, I'm *sorry*. I'm just here to tell you that you aren't getting any of your stuff back. You've got to go someplace new, start over. You will never go home again," says the stranger. He waits for you to say something, but you remain silent. He waits more. You have nothing to say, with no way to say it.

"Would you still want to know why?" he says.

"Why?" You know now that there can't really be a good reason, not one you can understand. Your mind is trying to defend itself, and has given you the sensation of looking down on yourself from above. The only things that will not scare you are things that happen to other people. It has stopped drizzling, but you are still very damp. The air is hot and humid, and clogs your lungs. Or that's how you would describe the feeling.

"Let's say life is a mountain range," says the stranger. "Some people stay at the base of the mountains, but some people try to scale them, because they think something better lies on the other side. You scaled the mountains, but you found out there were just more mountains. That's all there is, really. Mountains. It's goddamn mountains all the way down. So you just gave up. Set up a hut on a mountain or something. That doesn't have anything to do with the rest of it, but that's what you do. Anyway. There is no end to the mountains, but you're supposed to keep climbing. Until you die, you know. It doesn't matter if it ended happily. It doesn't matter if you died with regrets. The in-between stuff is the important part. Whatever legacy you were supposed to have. But you never did that."

"Th-that's total garbage," you say, "I don't have to leave some mark to be happy. I don't have to do anything."

"Well, fantastic, then!" he shouts, "You haven't left any mark at all! You can start over from the base of the mountains, or you can just rot there. Feel free." The stranger points to a huge pair of wire cutters that are now on the ground next to you. The handles are covered with fabric identical to your lost bag. You point to them and look up at the stranger, who makes a sour face and shrugs. You know that the stranger knows more than you. You don't trust yourself, so you stand limply and quietly, gaping. You don't have the guts to stand up for yourself or to admit you were wrong. You pick up the wire cutters and begin the tedious business of making a hole in the fence. How did you even think you would get out? You are certain the stranger is staring at you while you work, but you refuse to make eye contact. When you finish, you climb out, the wire scratching and poking you on every side. Then you shuffle slowly around, and leave. You imagine that maybe you will live in a cardboard box with a pile of blankets beneath an underpass. You will save up enough for bus tickets and travel wherever you can reach. You hope that you won't freeze at night when the temperature drops.

"So is this it, then?" asks the stranger.

"It is. You were, um, not helpful," you respond. Your eyes burn, and your mouth tastes like cooking chocolate, but you managed a retort. Poorly, but you did it. You don't look back at him, and you don't know if he can see you or not when you break into a jog. You wonder if you look stupid, but push that thought away. Nobody knows you, so who are you trying to impress? Air rushes through your ears, and you sweat in the heat.

After you are already gone, your friend walks up to the lot where your house once sat. She doesn't remember why she came, but thinks that coffee shop she likes might be down the street. She feels nothing, no déjà vu, no odd spark or stray thought. You keep running, and it takes much longer than usual for you to run out of breath. Your friend realizes that she was thinking of a different coffee shop.

UNTITLED

Bella Masterson

Aristotle, *noun,* Greek philosopher. Famous quote: "The whole is greater than the sum of its parts."

When I was young, I thought I was going to be a veterinarian. I went to farm camp in an Amish town in Ohio and collected eggs and milked goats for one blissful week each summer. Aristotle said that the gender of goats depends on which way the wind is blowing. At age nine, with young human hands on old goat udders, I knew this wasn't true. Aristotle said that the heart, not the brain, is the center of intelligence. At age nine, I hadn't yet proved this false. Aristotle said that everything is forgotten through time. Even at age nine, I disagreed.

Chuck Taylors, *noun,* the name for a pair of shoes developed by Converse.

I recently stumbled upon a photo of a three-year-old me wearing baby pink Converse high tops. I glanced down at my feet to see a scuffed pair of bright red Converse high tops. I have had a pair of Chuck Taylors at every time in my life. Black, bright white, off-white, navy, black, skull-patterned, camouflage print, splatter-paint, monogrammed, yellow, black, and now red. I would wear them with dresses, with a tie-dye shirt and camouflage print pants, and during every style phase of my adolescent life. My mom grimaces at the lack of arch and ankle support, but they were the only brand I would wear for much of my life.

iPod Shuffle - 2nd generation, *noun,* a portable electronic device for playing and storing digital audio files.

I grew up on The Beatles, so obviously the most amazing Christmas gift I ever got was one from my godfather; a clip-on 2nd generation iPod shuffle that my dad had already pre-loaded hundreds of songs onto. At this point in my life, the only technology I had experienced was solitaire on my dad's flip phone or the Harry Potter computer game on an ancient desktop computer in the basement. That whole day I listened to The Beatles on shuffle, and only turned it down when my sister said she could hear my music from "all the way across the room!"

Katharine, *noun,* a name.

My claim to fame in middle school was that I was a "test-tube baby." I would tell this to kids on the playground and wait for their reactions to switch from surprise to confusion, to awe. When they asked what it meant, I would tell them that a woman named Kathy gave birth to me (my middle-namesake), but I was still 100% my mom and dad's kid and I was not adopted. This made me feel incredibly cool, and while eventually other kids lost interest and realized that it was not, I would still proudly tack it onto my introductions. "I'm Bella… did you know that I'm a test-tube baby?"

Migraines, *noun,* a recurrent, throbbing headache that is often accompanied by nausea and disturbed vision.

Migraines are, regrettably, hereditary, although my mother never warned me that they would be as bad as they are. My first migraine made me feel as though "my head was splitting open, my stomach had detached from my body, and my eyes were on fire." I found that in an old diary a couple of years ago, and the hyperbole is warranted. I used to get them every few weeks, and lay with my eyes closed and a damp washcloth on my forehead for hours. I don't get them that often anymore.

Pacifier, *noun,* a rubber teether for a baby to suck on.

As a baby, I slept with one pacifier in my mouth and five in the bed around me. When one would fall out, I would scream until my flailing arms found another in the bed. After pacifiers, my next oral comfort was sucking my thumb, which then gave way to biting my nails, which then evolved into picking my nails, which I still do. My parents tried everything to get me to stop biting my nails as a child, from foul-tasting nail solutions to incentives and gifts as rewards. Nothing worked, and although I hated the look of my fingers and how they would always bleed, I did nothing to stop. My little brother bites his nails as well, and while he goes from one nervous habit to the next (chewing his cheek, twirling his hair), I don't bite my nails out of nerves - it's just a habit. Why is it so hard to break habits, even if there is no reason behind them?

Peppermint, *noun,* the cultivated Old World plant that yields peppermint leaves or oil.

Age eight, sitting in my parents' bathroom with my dad, we would rub peppermint lotion on our feet and scrape the bottom of our heels with his foot scrubber. According to organicfacts.net, peppermint tea can help with indigestion and pain relief, but it doesn't mention that it is the perfect cure for nostalgia. My psychology teacher says this is because olfactory information is processed near the memory processing parts of the brain, and I agree. Just one smell brings me back to my parents' bathroom, seeing remnants of my mother's lipstick on the wall from when my little sister tried to put makeup on her face.

Tears, *noun,* a drop of clear salty liquid secreted from glands in a person's eye when they cry.

I cry all the time - sad tears, happy tears, confused tears, stressed tears, nervous tears, love tears, defeated tears. My sister cried when she sees homeless people under the bridge in the winter. My brother cries when he is frustrated with his friends. My mother cried when Brian Johnson got kicked out of AC/DC. My nana cried when she read our Christmas card.

Violin, *noun,* stringed musical instrument of treble pitch played with a horsehair bow.

Age five, my first violin lesson, chubby fingers grabbing my kleenex-box "violin," imagining myself playing "Twinkle, Twinkle Little Star" onstage like my big sister. Imagining myself getting flowers afterwards from my grandma and a tin jar of cookies from my nana. A few years later, my best friend would tell me that the bow is made out of a horse's hair and an elephant's tusks, and that he didn't believe that a vegetarian should be playing an instrument made out of animal parts. I'm still a vegetarian and I still play an instrument made out of animal parts.

GOOD FRIDAY

Cristina Cass

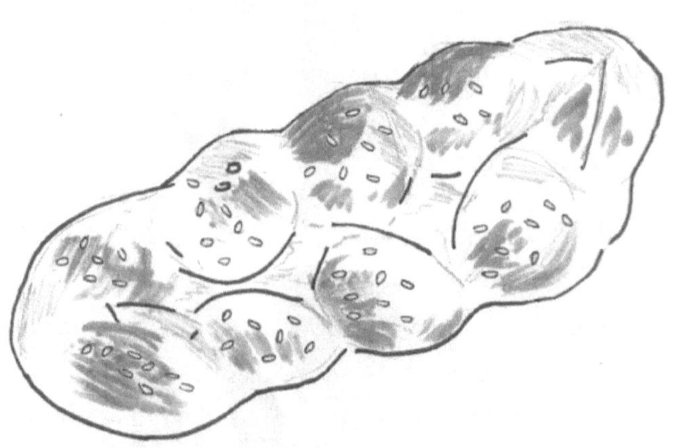

On Good Friday, Mama and Auntie Karineh made *choereg*. They braided the little loaves as the sunlight streamed through the kitchen window, bouncing off the blue and yellow tiles to light their faces. Lily sat on one of the leather-covered bar stools, watching them with her dark eyebrows furrowed. The smell of meat and spices and nearly-baked pastries threatened to take her back to the mythical homeland she had never seen, but she fought it. With all her ten-year-old strength, she fought to stay grounded in America, in her world of pizza and fourth grade and North Face fleeces. She got up reluctantly when her mother asked her to get the black caraway from the pantry.

Lily spoke barely above a whisper as she padded towards the pantry in her pink bunny socks. "None of my friends make *choereg*."

Aunt Karineh looked at her sister. Anahit sighed and turned to her daughter.

"Your grandpa Ara," she said, "Was a genocide survivor."

Lily remembered grandpa Ara. He had died when she was four, but she held on to bits and pieces of his memory. The smell of spices and cigars and Armenian brandy. His white beard and silver cross pendant. And one word. "*Hayaghjik.*"

As Mama began to tell her story, Lily couldn't help being pulled back in time, to a two-story house with intricate Armenian rugs on every floor. A family of five eating *lavash*, the traditional Armenian flatbread, before their Good Friday dinner. An ominous clamor outside brought Tamar to the four-paned front window. She looked outside, then back at her husband. The fear jumped from Artur to his son Ara, to Suzanna and little Nune like an electric charge.

"What is it?" Artur asked.

Tamar couldn't get past the knot in her throat to answer, but her husband already knew. They had thought about making plans for months now, but with the slow-footed reluctance of people who couldn't imagine needing them, they hadn't made any.

Artur got up. "Out the back door," he said. "Now."

Tamar's maternal reflexes kicked in as she grabbed a roll of *lavash* and her nine-year-old daughter, and ran.

Ara followed his older sister Suzanna under the apricot tree and into the field behind their house. He looked back at his his bedroom window, calling out to him from the second story. He wished he could have taken his book. He felt Suzanna's hand pulling at his and turned back around. Neither of his parents had looked back, but it was already too late. They heard a shout from behind them.

"Ermeni!" A gruff voice shouted at them in Turkish. The soldier's mustachioed face scowled at them. He was looking at Tamar, and Nune, who held on tightly to her mother's hand. Ara's eyes were glued to his little sister, but Suzanna knew what was happening, so with a choking sob she gathered her resolve and ran. Ara felt himself pulled behind her, and turned away.

They ran as fast as they could towards the orchard, their last hope. The soldier's shouts followed them as they ran into the trees, but years of hide and seek led them to a little cave hidden by bushes and fallen tree branches. Nune's favorite hiding spot.

Lily looked up at her mother. Anahit had fallen silent. It was Aunt Karineh who broke the silence.

"We make *choereg* on Good Friday to remember Tamar and Artur and little Nune, and all the hateful, angry people who made sure that they would never make *choereg* again. We make *choereg* to meet that hatred and anger with pride, and love. We make *choereg* because we are Armenians—we're survivors. Understand, *Hayaghjik*?"

There was that word again. *Hayaghjik*. My Armenian girl.

UNTITLED

Daniel Dardon

You said that everything was okay.
You lied.

Potential was oozing like the inside of a volcano's magma
chamber.
That would soon overflow and run down its rigid sides.
That no man-made object could destroy.
That only nature's barriers could hold.
Just like good Transcendentalists might argue.
You, I believed.

You said that we could go to new heights under your leadership.
There would be no flat tires or broken brakes.
That there would be no shortage of fuel on your watch.
You and your bullshit are getting old.

Looks like you don't know that you're also quite careless.
You saw the fuel gauge draw near empty and didn't bother to
refill.
Did you not have any gas or did you lack the drive?

You never had a warranty and it was all hogwash.
Now we're just before the finish line and can't move.
It's a dead end with one way out.
We hop out and go our separate ways.

I'm not upset with you nor do I hate you.
I pity you.
You may ask why am I not upset.
Grandma always said "Don't hold grudges."

We can revisit this another time if you don't have it in you to
apologize.
But before I go I would like to apologize.
I apologize for placing so much trust in you.

P.S.
Sorry if the analogies and images throw you for a loop—
I expected you to be able to comprehend

EMPTY AIR

Franny Weed

You are driving down the highway, judging by the wind.

When we weren't tall enough to fight for shotgun, you'd always roll down both our windows in the back seat. You were the only one who liked the way the wind beat against the open car, amplifying our silence with the way the air thumped through all the space between the bodies in the car. And then you'd stick your head out of the window and let the wind's weight push your neck back against the window sill. And as you'd smile, your mouth would go dry and your cheeks would harden, until somebody would threaten to cut your head off if you didn't close the window.

I'm calling you now to ask for a little more time. A month, a week, at least a few days.

You must remember how I used to stick my head out of the window, too. My hair, always longer, would get stuck, tangled in the speed of the air, but my mouth would be open and my laughter so loud that my tongue would go dry. We'd hold hands across the space of the back seat of that old green car, clutching tightly so we wouldn't fly out. And sometimes our hands would get too sweaty, so we'd wipe them off on the peeling leather seats and go right back to holding, pushing our legs out straight, until our chests pressed the glass closer to the desert lining the sides of the highway.

And the car would stop and somebody'd threaten to not buy us lunch if we didn't sit down, but our throats were too empty to respond so we just pressed our heads to our knees to put the blood back in our brains. But we still held hands, at least until the air, now sealed in the car, became stale.

And all I'm asking for is a little more time. The money I owe, it'll come, I promise– just give me a month or two. No more.

I swear it's so near, just a second from my grip, paper cutting my finger tips. And we will laugh like we did then, we will lose our breath.

But you say you don't remember our breath gone. You say you remember my waist hitting the window sill as you grabbed my arm, you remember me going out too far one time and the wind holding the driver's screams. And my other arm reaching to catch the wind while my throat closed around the empty air. You say I wanted the wind that wasn't so close to the car, the wind running on the place where the highway met the desert, the wind that would cut my mouth with sand. You remember our heads leaning out of the windows until my hand slipped to wipe on the leather seats and didn't reach back for yours.

REVELATIONS FOR A NUCLEAR AGE

Gabe Hatto

He was very small in front of the console— so small as to be but an ant before a wise and calculating God. With gloved hands above his head, he bent his visored gaze to his boots and wept. Falling to his knees, he prostrated himself. Deliver me, O Lord, deliver me from the world and its sinners, from the ills and aches of the world, from nuclear War and freezing nuclear Death, from Radiation and from Plague, and from the infernal machines of Man.

In a voice like the fraying string of a violin, he pleaded, and so it came about that the angel Barak heard his call. With a shriek of wind and snowy ash, the crackling messenger of the Hashmalim bent his body through the first monitor and reached gray hands to cradle the face of the small man. Barak spoke in a voice like faraway thunder, from furnace-lungs and through static storms, his voice blowing in sheets of lightning and illuminating his long gray face from within in a radiant firestorm.

"Why have you come to this place, my son?" Words leapt from graveyards of blunted teeth, jittering through the skull of the other man and popping into his consciousness like a memory long-forgotten but once remembered.

"Barak," he said, "I have come to ask a boon. Why have the thoughts of man turned to waste and what lies beyond it, that terrible and endless Abyss of bone and ice? Why have the days of man become an endless night of deep clouds and dark hideaways?" Barak thought long and hard, his long delicate fingers rolling tap-tap across his jutting chin. Coming not to a conclusion, he sat cross-legged with the man and began to pray with him, a buzzing synthesizer, cross-checked and hooked into a great Amplifier accompanied by a wavering squeal of horsehair on gut wire.

*   *   *

With a click-clack symphony of pistons and switches, the great hands of Ehud reached through the second monitor, planting themselves fully on the ground and pulling a great potbellied satellite-body into the room. Camera-eyes looked down benevolently from a squat Shali face, and Ehud bent down to rest on his heels next to the proud angel and the cowering man. He spoke in a voice like a thousand dial tones;

"What has Man to ask in this age of provision and comfort? Brother, lie not by the side of bio-purism and regression." The man looked up with angry eyes and cried out against the great metal harbinger.

"Honored Messenger of Shaliyim! Answer me how this age is one of comfort when billions lay starving in languid trenches or filthy holes, when they slaughter each other for meat or scrap, for a bomb shelter or a woman? Answer me how it is just that those who live in networks and wires, ones and zeros, refuse enlightenment to the poor and the needy? Why has Man become so cruel?"

Great teeth ground against each other, and a droning whine of processors at work became audible. Ehud tapped his fingers against his cranium rhythmically, and somewhere far away, the fluorescent lights in a small buried room burnt out abruptly. After an amount of time, Barak laid his spidery hand on Ehud's shoulder and said, "Brother, I cannot find the way of it either. It is beyond my ken why there is no hope for Man." So

the three sunk to their knees on the steel-paneled floor
and wailed in a symphony of oscillating sine waves and
raw human crisis.

And from the third monitor leapt Hadar, spry carbon talons
landing in curls of steel on the cold floor. His body positively
pulsed with energy, the burning nuclear heat at his core giving
his bone-white cheeks a ruddy sheen and lighting up his eyes
with a spark of fission. He looked at the three figures on the
floor uneasily, and cried out to the prostrate trifecta.

"Why have you lowered yourself so, Brothers? Why, man, have
you consorted with
Malachim and yet are
not glorious yourself?"
The two angels turned
to the Seraph and away
from the weeping man
and, standing, spoke in
words of icy multitudes,
colonies buried in
sweeps of ashy gray
flakes and illuminated
by blinking terminal
cursors.

"Hadar!" they cried. "Surely you must be able to answer this
man's question! Why has Man fallen so, to wars and strife and
the destruction of what he once held dear?"

Hadar pondered the query, his head wreathed in radioactive
steam and his perfect brow furrowed in first doubt. His

face turned again to his audience, and his voice rung out like the striking of a great bell, his breath like the sound of a hundred bombers overhead and his words like the coughs of combustion chambers.

"Brothers," he said, "I do not know for why I fight, but I know that I must. There is some order to it, this I know, but I cannot glean my reason." He thought again, his mind a cavern of thundering jackboot-thoughts, and cast his eyes to the man on the floor. He looked again at his brother Malachim, and rested his hand on the man's shoulder. The three sank to their knees again, and this time a third voice joined their chorus, a red cry of brothers lost to darting lead, a symphony in the key of strife.

The Aether was crowded by now, milling with a thousand tiny angels, and so it happened that the mournful voices of the four rang out in such a great din that they touched each corner of

the seven realms. The fourth monitor began to glow dully, and great footsteps could be heard, thunderous and weary, a worn mountain heaving itself into motion. They ground like stone on stone, and out from the terminal of the monitor folded a great gray body, a face like a craggy outcropping lined by aeons, hands like articulate tectonic plates, eyes wise and sorrowful with time. As one, the Malakim pressed their faces to the floor and silenced themselves. The man was suddenly aware of a presence, a giant the size of the universe somehow bending down to him and cradling him in its arms.

"My son," it said. "What has become of thee?" A voice that ought to have leveled mountains with a mere syllable spoke to him then, with the gruff tenderness of a father and the assuredness of the purely right. He looked up, and suddenly he could do no more than weep, his voice giving way and his eyes clouding with tears. "My son," the voice said again, and sighed like a storm petering into blue sky. "I know what thou hast to ask; thy need not say. But, my son, I have naught to do with it. I am old now, and it is not for me to give the wherefore of the world, nor is it for me to give the order of every event. It is for my eternal and self-fathering son. The world is Man's."

He was set on the floor again, his body trembling as, mournfully, He stepped through the screen and into oblivion again. Hadar looked back at him with downcast eyes, coals burning slow and red, as he disappeared into the third monitor. Ehud chittered to himself, low, and climbed through the second screen, a quick sad last glance his only memento. And Barak wrapped a long arm around the man's shoulders as he sat on the floor, sharing silence with the wayward soul as the glow of the screen softly played across their faces. With a whisper of cold wind and the soft sounds of muted wasteland rockfalls, he stood, skeletal and gray. Folding himself again into bright light, he looked back with penitent orbs to meet the lonely gaze of the man on the floor. Wordlessly, he turned, and vanished.

And Man was alone again.

ENCOUNTERS

Imaan Yousuf

One of my many skills is completely fixating on first encounters with people. While I do enjoy reliving some of the better executed first-time encounters, I know for a fact that I'm particularly good at never letting go of the terrible ones. They leave me drained and completely dissuaded from ever pursuing further encounters with that person. UGH. I'm almost certain I said something stupid. And if I can't immediately recall my highlight reel of bad conversation moments, I take my time mulling it over until I can find something that makes me want to floss the incorrect way. Why does popular culture want us to believe that flossing is the act of painfully pulling the floss back and forth, like some rusty pulley system, in your mouth? No. Carefully pluck between each tooth.

Now that I'm taking psychology in school, I understand that

I'm not some rare breed of human (hard for me to hear as a teenage girl). We all tend to focus on the bad. That explains why every first-time encounter/social encounter feels like a completely misguided tattoo. It's definitely full of regret.

I concentrate really hard. I don't half-ass my fastidious examination of past events. If I'm gonna do it, I'm gonna give it my all. I like to apply this work ethic to all things in life. What did I say? How misshapen were my words? How about theirs? Were we equally bad at having the conversation? Maybe, but I'll take full responsibility for the orphaned pauses that no one else seemed to want to claim.

CAITLIN TAKES A BIG OL' BITE

Imaan Yousuf

We were at the height of our Andersonville playgroup days. On this particular Wednesday morning, we were walking back from Storytime at Women and Children First. Cathy read us *The Hungry Caterpillar* again, but we didn't mind because we loved Eric Carlson's illustrations. Hilda and Ruth were walking two steps behind us, making sure we didn't try and run into Erikson's for a pretzel stick without permission, because then we would ask if they could buy us Baby Bell cheeses, and that would definitely spoil our Chef Boyardee Beefaroni lunches.

That day was extra special because Haila was spending the day with me, and I didn't think there was anything more impressive than me having a friend who was a whole two years older than me. She was in school! She knew how to venture into the abyss that awaited after number lines that stopped at ten.

For some reason, I wanted to throw Haila in your face and make you jealous. I guess I was that despicable (just call me Gru!), but then again, I was under the age of seven and free of the guilt that comes with having morality. You made me pay for my actions, though. After relentlessly going on and on about the fun I would have with Haila at Giraffe Park, you bit me. You took my left forearm and you bit me. No meager cheese-tasting bite– a big ol' hearty bite of juicy, brown Imaan steak. The tears came immediately. I was sure– and still am– that I accomplished my mission of making you jealous of my other friendship.

Today, you deny the allegations that you bit me out of jealousy and spite, but we both know that you're living a lie. It was not just a biting phase. No, this was one significantly individual bite. Even after all these years, when you don't actively seek my forgiveness, I give it to you. You've been a better friend than Haila ever could be, and I'm sorry I thought otherwise over ten years ago. I hope you can forgive me.

DAIRY

Imaan Yousuf

Dairy

I give you permission

Wreck my stomach

So long as I can have the pleasure of pulling apart your
    stringy mozzarella sticks

I prefer not to have you in your weakened, limp,
    room-temperature state

But I will still nurture you and pull you apart with care

I will tentatively bite into the waxy skin of your round, full

Brie figure (always temporarily forgetting if it's edible)

I will resign myself to amazement every time I discover your
    simultaneously sweet and salty character

I will drink your calcium-rich nectar, known as "milk" by
    common folk, hoping to find my strength in its
    nutritional value

You only have one serious flaw that I think you are very
    well aware of

You sit in the hands of Jamie Lee Curtis

Telling the world how good you are for digestive systems
Or let Bobby Flay get you to the Greek and use you as a
    substitute in cooking
No! I see right through you to your tartness and tang, and I
    almost hate you for letting yourself regress to a yogurt form
You're so much better than that
Don't let the world manipulate you
You're cultured enough without bacterial fermentation
Oh, dairy. You always trick me into thinking you're good for me,
    but I end up sick and gassy in the end.

I think you're worth it.

BACKYARDIGANS

Kendall Roberts

He is right in front of me

I'm brown butter pecans and he is peanut color mixed
with cream fluff

Why does he speak in tones that dissect themselves between
propellers, like r's that roll off my American/Southern
tone tongue.

Why is it here?
the *Amor* risen with praised, crossed hands stuck in a
batholith, parting two cultures...
Apartheid.
That starts with....He is right in front of me

I'm brown butter pecans and he is peanut color mixed
with cream fluff

Why have we been blocked by the batholith?
A large gate that intruded in the form of stone.
Cemetery of weeds formed to take mass incarceration.
The shards of rainbow reflective glass thrown by women
    and men, laid flat at the first line.

We are first in line.

To see them get crushed and turned into the colored
Amen

Magic

Amazed he's the boy in the striped pajamas?
A smokehouse away.
Five blocks.
Would I face misjudgement, and a slap on the hand to
    never cross a border?

Ask mommy, "Why can he?"

and never realize he couldn't.

How does his grandmother have 21-year-old legs?
That walk corners.
Making sure her grandson wouldn't become outline or
    graffiti imprint that crossed hands would watch.

Why would he become outline?

What's that smell?

We smell at a safe distance through windows sealed?
With secrets

Which secrets?

The smell of slaughter?

Or

What's slaughter?

Something that wasn't used in my backyard– neither his– but
in front of sealed windows.

Why didn't we know front?
Unless it was school seen through window seal?

What's the big secret?

That he didn't know playpen
Five blocks away with that smell.

What's the big secret?
That I didn't know pen
resting in the rainbow reflective glass.

I guess it blinded both of our eyes not to fall for it.

To intrude our direction from....

If we ever touched hands, would it match the praised ones
    that looked upon us?

That precious blood thinking that playing paddy cake
    would leave hands damaged?

With ground.

Or

Each other.

We've been blocked by

Why didn't he want greens touching avocados?

Green is green to kids
As black was to love
As hispanic was to *amor*

As slaughter was to precious blood.

Is that the secret?

What's misjudgement?

Separating sides of precious blood that can end up becoming

What's that smell?

It's slaughter.

That he's right next to me?

That I'm brown butter pecans

and he's peanut color mixed with cream fluff

That if a move was to be made

Lithification would take over

hands might be damaged from sharp pricks that went
   with praised crossed hands stuck in concrete

My hands shook his anyway
with no slap on the wrist
concretion is no longer the love or *amor*.

Mom, is it just concrete?

TORN

Kendall Roberts

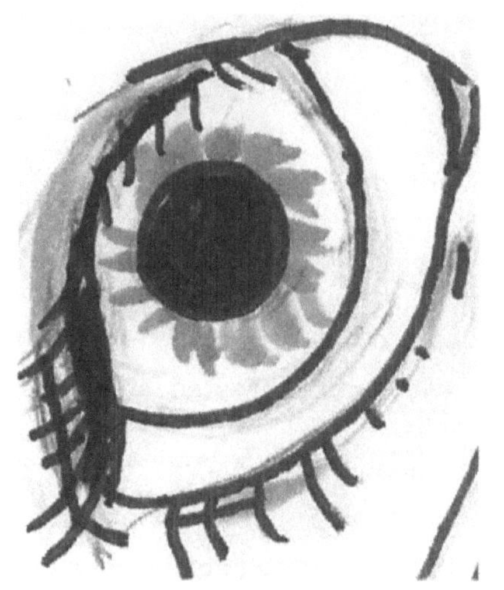

I don't speak.

Most people think normally and connect with each other, but I... I just keep everything in my big brain, hoping that it doesn't explode and everyone plays jigsaw with it.

It feels wrong when someone tells you that you have no voice.

No solace to settle wounded thoughts.

Maybe it was supposed to be a big push-off ledge. They thought they were helping you fall into the mist of perception, but they never saw the aftermath.

I mean, I don't think soft pillows are supposed to feel like dead weight. You're made to fly like a butterfly and sting like a bee, a bee with no stinger.

Be morphed.

Slowly but surely, pollen would have to rub off on you if you stay with it, right?

Or maybe mutation would just take over.

I know the special ones get haunted by the nicest kids in town,
I know....

One two it's coming, three four have back bone, five six don't
step on cracked curves that will break teen spirit, seven eight
reality got you ate seven eight, 8 reality is just a matter of
perception. Reality and perception a cornucopia of clashing,
divergent ideas. Classic case of what is and isn't in the mind,
yet they don't want you to keep searching reality, they want
you to stay in the twilight zone.

With hopes to reach out to the stars, pipe dreams that heart
wouldn't be crushed by meteor. Instead it showered and made
me feel like impossible girl.

Turned stone cold

You still have to play monkey see, monkey do.

Still have questions like, if they could copy me, why would
they need me?

Those thoughts run through my head; of them not wanting and
feelings of what's wrong...with me

Am I not skeleton hidden well enough behind perfect
white smile?

When every bone starts to be put in closet, hidden with key,
and still gets hit with erosion. The madness will never arise to
them that maybe they were a part of the burial.

Every tear that I cry would be out of frustration that I wouldn't
any longer be colorful yellow or gold.

I would just have:

The bluest eyes, the bluest eyes, the BLUEST EYES,
THEBLUEEYES, THE BLU-EST EYES,

And be stuck like this.

They don't need to speak when they have hair spray to keep
them mounted high. They don't have big noses, wide hips, love
handles, and would purge if someone even drank a milkshake
in front of them.

Why can't I look in the mirror and see what they see?

I mean, I believed that beauty was in the eye of the holder, but
what happens when they are not yours to begin with?

When those eyes just make you want to go silent.That's why
I don't speak.

When your inner hate never disintegrates and you dismember.

Mother knows best, society wants to contest, and me?

I DON'T KNOW ABOUT MYSELF ANYMORE.

ODE TO SOCK DUDE

Lillie Therieu

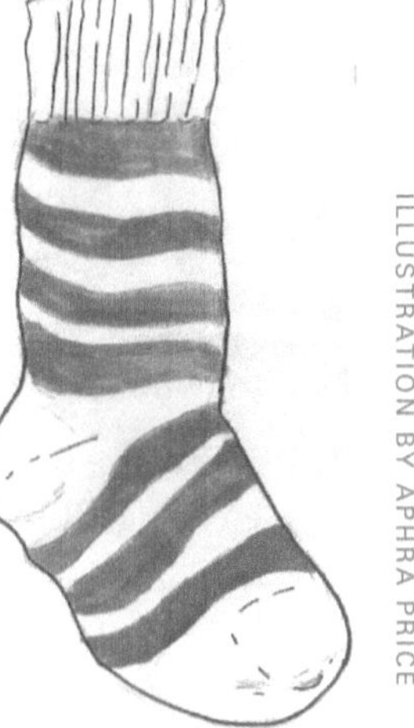

"i've been a senior for three years"
he tells me with gap teeth and a roll of twenties
but he's making more cash than any college kid i know
he's a high school ENTREPRENEUR

sock dude educates me about the free market
"this is the best goddamn country."
he whistles "proud to be an american"
listening to sock dude is way better than reading *das kapital*
sock dude is the o.g. capitalist

he has a gooood advertising campaign going
giant bulky trench coat fresh outta *that's so raven*
so conspicuous that no one will ever call him out

he spreads the two sides like wings
christ the redeemer
a god amongst men
the coat is lined with socks in bright neon lines
sock dude is better than the neon sign store
five bucks a pop; for the socks and the spirit

each one's a saintly relic man

hallelujah grown up jesus

he steals 'em from the dollar store
everyone knows

sock dude is rollin in free money
he's got a 500% profit margin
he's savvy he's thrifty he's rangey
he's seemingly unaffected by the collapsing economy

(THEY SAY HE SELLS DRUGS, TOO, BUT IT'S A SIDE
HUSTLE; THE SOCKS BRING THE REAL MONEY)

sock dude's got the soul of the city
he's tamale man
he's the political machine
he sells oregano to freshmen
he sells ten dollar tacos to drunk tourists
sock dude creates supply and demand

when sock dude graduated he was mourned
was eulogized
was honored by every kid with something to sell and nothing
to lose
he was a pillar of the community
he taught me survival
smiled pure business
and preached no one's got a monopoly on smart
high school is real world
and sock dude was ceo shark tank kingpin genius

STRANDBEESTS

Lucie McKnight

I would love to see them on the sand.

Against a gray-blue background of the North sea, a wild Lake Michigan on a grand scale. They exist within the stagnant hall, mimicking the fossils they were based upon. The creaking of their plastic bones echoes around wood details and bounces off the glass walls, trapping the noise, instead of it being swallowed by a crashing wave.

The beasts represent a prehistoric modernity, something organic made with electricity rather than evolution, with soft canvas skin and sharp corners. Nothing like them has existed in a thousand years. They move with surprising personality despite being nothing more than a skeleton, and their speed is unexpected. Instead of a slow, mammoth, prehistoric pace, the beasts find their energy in bursts, shuffling and creaking and crying for a second of consolidated movement then dragging to a stop, powered by the shift of the wind and any compressed air the gentle giants can hold within themselves.

The most shocking thing is the noise they make. It doesn't sound artificial or plastic, it sounds like something ancient, like a sleeping dragon extending its wings for the first time in a long time.

It feels more awake than most people, more alive than most animals. It's energy fills up the space. They are declared extinct, by the author himself, but I've never seen a fossil move with such intensity.

DISNEYLAND

Lukia Artemakis

searching in closets

for pockets of poems I wrote in sixth grade

on the playground where I roamed and stayed all afternoon

recess always ending too soon

now I fan out pictures on hardwood

laughing at how candid I was

how stranded I was

on an island alone with my own notions

alone on an ocean of thought

only the buzz

of my hopes plain and laid out like clothes out of the dryer

like the fanned out pictures where I see the liar

the person who claimed she foresaw what she stood for

what she was good for

now she has a cloudy past

and a cloudy cup of tea

one tea bag if I'm fast

two tea bags if I'm in a hurry

folded corners of off-white copy paper

she stumbles to class

her vision's cloudy and blurry

her flag half-mast
her school is a sea
and she hates it because she's trying to flee
and so far from where she wants to be
rhyming the letter 'e'
when she used to know her powers of three
now she uses a calculator
somehow still wanting to be an educator
like when she was a kid
they kid that she's still a kid

too long spent waiting for her own presence
reminiscence replaces her own essence
she's gotten under her own skin
and she's discovered it's paper thin
that lack of courage is
natural for kids your age
why is the teen committed to self-complacence?
I am to myself just an acquaintance

life used to be less about what you did in your spare time,
now I share time with my future
apparently he's my latest greatest suitor
I thought I'd understand myself forever

now I can't stand the noise, but I fool myself
  thinking I'm clever
I'm still that person
my mother and her son, my brother
still call me that name
it's the same name I used to blame for getting
  tricks played on me
in sixth grade. see?

I NEED SPACE

Lukia Artemakis

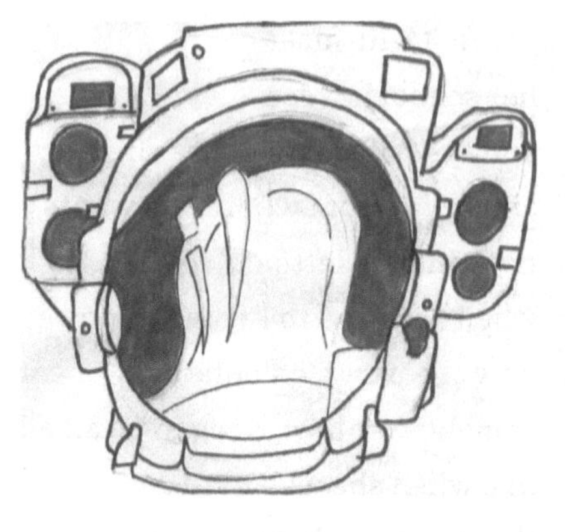

"Oh, shit."

A pause, followed by thirteen repetitions of that same exclamation. Parker wasn't some swearing lunatic unversed in an appropriate variation of the English language. His swearing was warranted several times by the following chain of events.

1. The handle of the main fuel valve had broken, releasing an amount of fuel that could get a JetBlue flight to Singapore from New York into space, never to be seen again (by humans, at least).

2. Fortunately, the spaceship had been equipped for this scenario, and oxygen was withdrawn from the tanks and converted into hydrogen, enough to fuel us home.

3. Unfortunately, our oxygen tanks had already sustained one hit this trip.

"Oh, shit." That's the fourteenth one in a minute, this time coming from me. That must be a record in space. (Everything's a record in space.) "Do the math, Parker." I meant to say it seriously, but it felt like a whisper. Sound travels differently when floating in a tin can. The barrel-shaped room had little in the way of acoustics. There wasn't even a flat surface to stand on. I wonder if NASA did that on purpose, removing everything that kept us grounded.

I locked eyes with him. I was the Mission Documentor, the English teacher with decent writing skills who thought she'd be hearty enough to survive in space. My technical job was to record and describe the conclusions Parker made from his physics experiments that required leaving objects in space and orbiting the planet until we reached them again. The mission, I knew, was about observing the corrosion and rusting patterns of substances for future spaceships. Although uneventful and routine, Parker got a kick out of his work. We once returned to an aluminum can we had left six months earlier that was now only recognizable as a ball the size of a penny, rusted to a deep brown. He pulled the unrecognizable ball back into the ship, and with awe under his breath, uttered that word that we had butchered fourteen a minute earlier.

In that second, I wish I had Parker's math degree, despite my unadulterated hatred for algebra. He had ripped a sheet off a clipboard that contained now useless instructions on how to set the clock on the main screen. Forcing his long blonde bangs back with his fingers, his eyebrows crinkled into a straight line. He scribbled with such ferocity, the hissing friction of the lead on the paper was the only sound in the ship. He was nervous, any man could've seen that, but he had to keep the pencil pressed hard to keep it from flying off the paper.

I didn't appreciate gravity while I was on Earth: not when I catapulted out of a tree at age seven, not in my feeble attempts at making my high school basketball team, and not when I passed out from the G-forces during the ascent into orbit. Humans have an obsession with getting off the ground, more than with our own survival. That's why the Wright Brothers flew a plane before Alexander Fleming invented antibiotics. Most people living on our blue speck don't even know who Fleming is.

Floating above the entire planet makes one seem powerful for the first few days. You are one of the few people in history who will be able to put the Earth and all its inhabitants between your thumb and your forefinger. The round windows are just like in the movies, and I spent days waiting for Earth to be exactly centered in the pane of glass. But that self-awareness wears through your brain quickly, and you grow tired of yourself being free of that blue sphere, chained to the insides of a cylindrical prison. I never liked exercising, but my legs itched to move and I squirmed thinking of how much I wanted to run across a field. It was a strange thought considering that outside the ship was all of undiscovered space.

I used to be tethered to teaching. I thought I could make a difference in how young people think, but I saw the jaded faces stare up at me, lost in their own daydreams. The next year, I would feel the same glossed over eyeballs haunt me in different bodies. I guess it was only fair that they should dream because my mind drifted off as well. I would think about flying and how fulfilling yet carefree life is for the birds outside the school's window. I was certain an astronaut was the next best thing. I should've entered the Air Force; somehow it would've been safer shooting bullets than watching the escaping oxygen on the monitor.

Space is a void. A beautiful one, I'll give it that. Maybe my sporadic sleep schedule in darkness contributed to it, but when I felt the intrigue of the abyss pulling me, my stomach would turn over, thinking of how much variety my life at home had. The expanse of the universe is brilliant, but even stars and planets look mundane after thirteen months.

In space movies, there's always a solitary astronaut, but I was here with Parker, and that easy tranquility of death alone in space was not a possibility. We would have to watch each other call our family, holding back the tears the other person wasn't shedding. As an English teacher, I have an appreciation for the romance of just falling asleep into eternity. Death is not so foreboding without consequences or thoughts of others. With another human being, however, you're forced to acknowledge the tragedy about to occur. What last words do you say to a colleague of three years, especially with Houston listening in? Of all the things I wouldn't mind death being, awkward is not one of them. I don't think I'd mind the hallucinations that come with death by oxygen deprivation. It would be a nice distraction from reality. But then again, I thought being an astronaut would be a nice distraction from reality.

"523," Parker whispered.

Dumbly, I thought it was the oxygen wheezing out of the tanks when he first said it. It was more of a hiss than a whisper. I barely heard the three syllables escape from his lips.

"What?" I said out of pure confusion.

"523."

"I heard you. 523 what?"

"Hours."

"So…" I hung onto the word, my voice sweeping up like hot air. I didn't feel inclined to do the math at that tense moment. My thoughts were limp with images of my own perishing.

"Don't look so glum, Diana, we're going to be fine. It's a bummer we'll have to head home so quickly, though." Parker sighed, with the most conviction I've ever heard from him. What a typical astronaut response. Parker was made to drift between rocks and hold his head up. He was the type to be able to laugh and cry about human existence. I was the type to go on a two-hour space trek without a reason.

THE RED DAY

Makele Clemmons

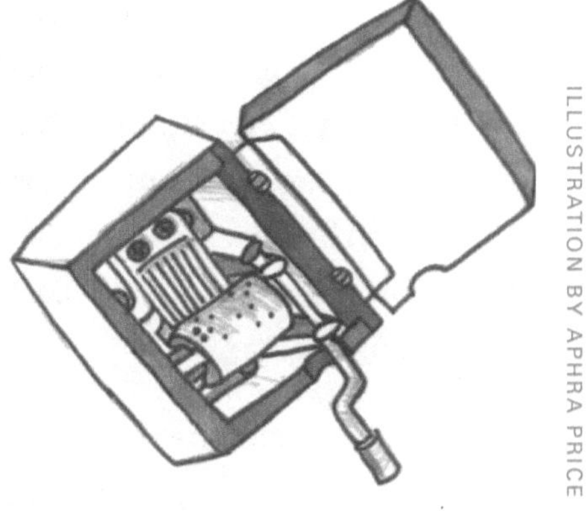

Red. My favorite color was red. As the red flames engulfed my childhood home, I could not stop thinking about my favorite things. There was the broken music box that played "Twinkle, Twinkle Little Star" in a cringeworthy key, every note flat– but only slightly. The chest full of crappy poems I wrote during my teenage angst phase. And worst of all, my very first guitar, Pif, crouched in a corner, littered in butterfly stickers. The red flames seemed to be waving goodbye. My mom, dad, and three siblings stood ironically frozen in place watching the flames. Standing in the dark of the night, our faces illuminated with red, my father was the first person bold enough to look at me. I could see the fire in his eyes. It was his eyes that said what everyone, including myself, knew. This is your fault.

Yes, I set my house on fire. It wasn't on purpose or anything, but it happened. It was my fault. I robbed my parents of the first house they'd ever owned and my siblings of their childhood home. I, too, was losing a large part of my life, but it was my fault. My loss seemed invalid. I was the villain in this story. Night to night I'd find myself reliving the red day. I could see the firefighters in their clunky boots, my home scribbled in red Crayola. I swear I could feel the heat of the flames mixing with the fall breeze. And then I would wake up drenched in sweat, cower into a question mark, and wait for my eyes to feel comfortable closing.

Months flew by and the fire within me began to cease. I experienced metamorphosis. My loose and liquid childhood solidified into an element foreign to me: adulthood. My childhood ended when I let go of the self inflicted guilt. It ended when I learned to evolve beyond the guilt. I realized that the past wasn't important. The past is just a story. A clumsy mistake should not be my definition. That is what I got out of the red day. I am more than a mistake. I am more than a default villain. I am more than the girl who burned down a house. I am human. I grow. I change. I evolve.

And now my favorite color is blue.

ENCOUNTERS

Tabitha DuBose

When I first saw you, I didn't know who you were. But then someone told me and I knew. I was able to put a face with a name, a face with a story– unfortunately, not the right story. And you knew of me. So then we knew about each other, without even officially meeting. Time went on, and we still just knew of each other, but we soon came face-to-face. We seemed comfortable with one another. We weren't necessarily friends, more like friends of a friend. But we still smiled when we came across each other, and I was doing most of the smiling because of the way you said my name. I know now that we both had a sudden interest in each other, but kept it to ourselves. More time passed, and there were times we'd engage in small talk. Still not so much friends, but definitely acquaintances. Later in the year, we meet again. This time we're pretty much friends. We have actual conversations, there are jokes being told, laughter, and so on. And eventually we exchange numbers.

LET ME BE YOUR TARGET

Tabitha DuBose

Hi, my name is Tabitha DuBose
You may have seen my face before or come across my
   name once or twice
Maybe you did and you didn't notice, but that's all right,
   apparently I'm easy to miss
Easy to miss, and hard to find, people have said
I'm short, I'm quiet, and I stay out of people's way
The only thing that makes me hard to miss is that smile
   of mine
I always have a smile on my face, even when it's
   not intentional
"Tabitha, why are you always smiling?" people ask
"I don't know," I say, "why not?"
And why not?
I'm happy, for the most part
I'm healthy, kind of
And even though there's often a frown in my heart, it doesn't
   mean my face has to have one
No I'm not doing drugs,
And no, I'm not going to tell you what I was thinking about to
   make me smile this hard
Honestly, me smiling all the time might be a problem
Maybe it's a defense mechanism, I don't know
But if it makes me stand out, I'll smile my biggest smile

until my cheeks hurt
And when I massage my cheeks to make them feel better,
    I'll smile again
Because I don't want to be the girl that you look over
I want to be the girl that's staring you right in the face
    like a target
But instead of shooting me down, you pick me up
You make my day because my smile made you smile,
And now we're both a little happier.

SAILOR OF THE MOON

Yazmeen Pablo

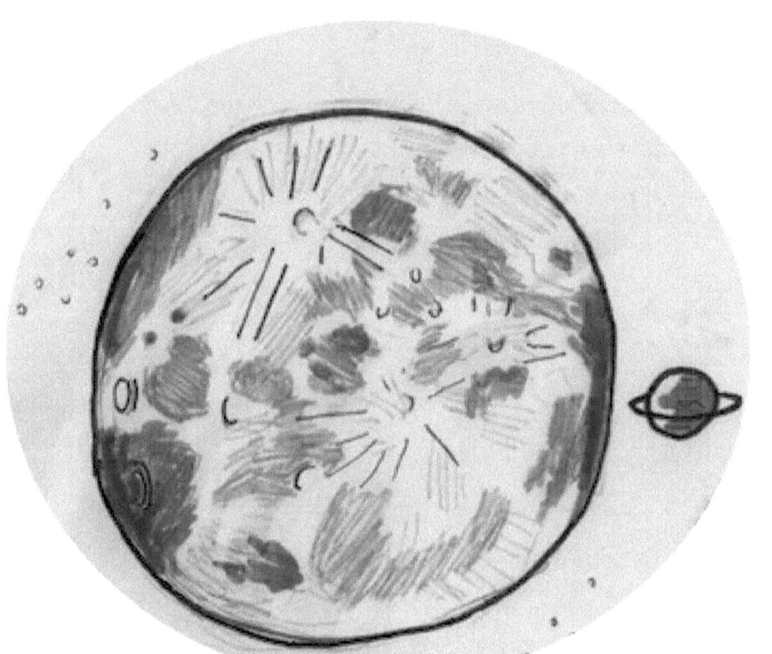

Sailor of the moon,

Cast a ship on the sea of my stars.

My lips of painted pink,

glitter streaks

Have your words cover me in darkness,

Express my shine

Soaring the skies like your eyes, blue,

Lines of green like pools,

They're shades darker than the others; like my hope.

Our colors met, you smiled

I am the skies and the ground,

You are the free roamer.

Your speeches teach my skies to glow,

But I still drown in my own

Seas from my eyes.

You are

my lover.

--DELETE--

Yellow and blue don't mix well,

That's what we are.

You keep up,

In my skies

And I keep down

In the cold water; tears

We're skies

And seas,

apart

Now you see I'm nothing but

sadness

AUTHOR BIOGRAPHIES

Aphra Price is a 15-year-old homeschooler, who is frequently filled with either righteous or arbitrary anger. Her favorite poem is "I Am The Only Being Whose Doom" by Emily Brontë, and while she does not have a favorite novel, she's currently very fond of *Slaughterhouse-Five* by Kurt Vonnegut. Aphra is wary of disturbing horror DVD cases, platitudes that apply to everyone ("This is the youngest that you'll ever be"), and the alleged flavor wildberry. Her all-time low score at laser tag is -329, under the nickname "saintjimmy" at a suburban Illinois LaserQuest.

Bella Masterson is a senior at Northside College Prep. She's been in YAB for four years and loves it. She is 17 years old, and has been a vegetarian for 12 years (or, ever since she saw her dad carving the Thanksgiving turkey and realized that eating meat actually meant eating animals). Today, her favorite book is *The Phantom Tollbooth* and her favorite movie is *Blue Velvet*. Yesterday she liked *Franny and Zooey* and *Austin Powers: International Man of Mystery*.

Cristina Cass is a junior at Whitney Young High School who loves reading novels, listening to Taylor Swift, and drinking tea. She has been writing historical fiction since her fascination with Ancient Greece as a six-year-old, but has taken an even greater interest in history ever since her recent trip to Armenia, 100 years after the Armenian Genocide that brought her family to America. She came back with a greater interest in her heritage, as well as an obsession with Armenian and Middle Eastern food. She is currently learning Armenian as her fourth language, but struggles with absurdly long words like *"tstesutyun"* (bye). In her free time she enjoys playing the guitar and baking, especially things with chocolate, and *choereg*, of course.

Daniel Dardon is a musician who walks the halls of Lane Technical College Prepatory High School. He aspires to one day succeed Gene Pokorny as the Principal Tubist at the Chicago Symphony Orchestra. He also dreams of attending Lawrence University in the near future. Daniel's days consist of him balancing academics, music, writing, and maintaining healthy relationships with family and friends. When he meets you, he sparks a conversation with you in hopes of putting not just a face to the name, but also a personality.

Franny Weed is 16 and doesn't have her driver's license yet, but is planning on getting it before her permit expires in August (she got her permit when she turned fifteen). She attends Francis W. Parker School and has been attending for six times the amount of time she's had her permit, plus a few months (12 years and nine months). Her favorite game is Haikubes (a Haiku dice game that is surprisingly unpopular). She has technically been involved in YAB since her freshman year of high school, but she doesn't like talking about that because she originally only went because she thought some of the then-juniors were cool and might be her friend if she saw them every other Monday. Now she comes to YAB because she's a cool junior with tons of every-other-Monday friends.

Gabe Hatto is sixteen-and-a-half years old and attends Northside College Prep. He likes H.P. Lovecraft and some of his imitators, indulges in China Mieville, and will be citing his Thomas Pynchon habit in his college applications. The newest album that's caught his eye is *Feelin Kind Free* by the Drones, but he can always come back to Boredoms and Nuno Canavarro. The margins of his papers are adorned with happy skeletons having a good time, as well as fish people, robots, and Cú Chulainn (the Thomas Kinsella translation of the Táin is very good). He's a new YAB member; he moved to Chicago from Dallas almost a year ago, and being in Chicago still tends to positively impact his ability to write sad stories. They're getting happier as he goes on, though.

Imaan Yousuf is a junior at Lane Tech and is *that* much closer to being a Dancing Queen. The anticipation is killing her but when it's finally that special day in May she will watch *Mamma Mia!* over and over again and have a dance party. (You're all invited! Just please remember to RSVP). She enjoys listening to the Ratatouille soundtrack and pretending she is well-versed in French music. She absolutely adores Marvin Gaye and Amy Winehouse, in no particular order. You can find her at home in her kitchen munching on what is supposedly "snacking chocolate," but is actually just broken pieces of dark chocolate, or in the basement pumping her legs with almost no resistance and embarking on a stationary bike expedition. Please don't ask her any technology-related questions because she takes too much pride in saying she is not tech savvy. Follow her on Twitter: @imaan_yo.

Kendall S. Roberts is 16 years old and was born and raised in the city of Chicago. She attends Simeon Career Academy on the South Side of the city. She is an activist, poet, artist, and aspires to be a Teaching Artist at a nonprofit organization called Young Chicago Authors. She is part of an organization called R.O.Y.A.L (Revolution of Young Artist as Leaders) in the Gresham-Auburn neighborhood at Cook Elementary School. Her favorite things to do are sleep, write, watch every movie with a rating under 40% on Rotten Tomatoes, thrift, and listen to very old music of all genres.

Lucie McKnight is 17 years old and a junior at Walter Payton College Prep. In her free time, Lucie loves walking around the city, reading, and writing stories that she has no intention of finishing. Lucie has been participating in 826CHI workshops since third grade, and this is her second year on YAB. She is so excited to be part of such an amazing group of people and to be featured in the chapbook.

Lukia Artemakis is 16 years old, and a junior at Whitney Young High School. She is an avid dancer and a member of Guys and Dolls Dance Company. When not dancing, she enjoys reading and writing short stories. She likes listening to Lorde and show tunes, with no in between. Recently, Lukia has explored photography, and has an obsession with photographing doorknobs. Although she isn't superstitious, she finds it hard to pick up the seventh Harry Potter book again after bragging that she's read it seven times in under seven hours. After high school, she hopes to combine her love of art and writing pursuing a career in Art Direction.

Makele Clemmons is 222 months old. She is a singer and songwriter at the Chicago High School for the Arts and plans to attend Berklee College of Music. Makele's dying wish is to meet Neil Patrick Harris and get a signed copy of "The

Playbook" from the hit TV series, *How I Met Your Mother*. Some of her accomplishments include: writing an entire musical score, eating three large pizza's in one day, being a master impersonator of Mr. Steal Yo' Girl, and attending the 58th annual GRAMMYs ceremony. I hear her hair's pretty cool, too.

Tabitha DuBose is now 18 years old, even though she doesn't totally look like it. She attends Wendell Phillips Academy High School, which she's only attended for two years, by the way. Tabitha's passion is writing— she loves it so much that she plans to make it her profession, starting at Columbia College in the fall. She also loves to bake, but that's just on the side for now. When she's not writing or baking she's usually deep into a movie or TV show, completely analyzing it and its characters. When you meet Tabitha, you remember her smile. She might be a little quiet, but that smile will definitely stick with you.

Lillie Therieau is a junior at Lane Tech who joined YAB because she loves being part of a community of writers and giving back to her city. Her passions include Haruki Murakami books, buttering toast, and old dogs.

Yazmeen Pablo is a fourteen-year-old freshman who is currently home educated. She likes to sit down and write as a way to escape. Her favorite book at the moment is *Gone Girl*, and she has grown fond of the writing style and the plot. She likes to read outdoors and on the train– places where it's quiet. She also enjoys all kinds of art, such as drawing and painting, while watching *Friends* all day.

ACKNOWLEDGMENTS

We are incredibly grateful for the generosity of our donors, who fund our programs and publications. Thank you for giving our students the opportunity to become published authors and share their stories with the world. You help them creatively engage with society at large; enriching the lives of our wider community of staff, families, school partners, volunteers, and readers.

ABOUT 826CHI

826CHI is a nonprofit organization dedicated to supporting students ages six to 18 with their creative and expository writing skills, and to helping teachers inspire their students to write.

Our services are structured around the understanding that great leaps in learning can happen with one-on-one attention, and that strong writing skills are fundamental to future success.

With this in mind, we provide after-school tutoring, creative writing workshops, in-schools support, help for English language learners, and assistance with student publications. All of our programs are challenging and enjoyable, and ultimately strengthen each student's power to express ideas effectively, creatively, confidently, and in their own voice. Learn more at: www.826chi.org.: www.826chi.org.

ABOUT THE WICKER PARK SECRET AGENT SUPPLY CO.

826CHI shares its space with the Wicker Park Secret Agent Supply Co—run by the neighborhood's only spy supplyists—which outfits its spy-entele with the latest and greatest in espionage wares. All funds raised through sales in the store support 826CHI's free programming.

Visit our brick-and-mortar shop at 1276 North Milwaukee Ave in Wicker Park to pick up a fresh grappling hook, trusty carrier pigeon, and weather-resistant notebook. You can also visit us online at: www.secretagentsupply.com.